BRIGHT and EARLY BOOKS
for BEGINNING Beginners

This book belongs to ...

_____

©Illus. Dr. Seuss 1957

GROLIER
BOOK CLUB EDITION

A Bright & Early Book

The Berenstain Bears
ON THE MOON

Stan and Jan Berenstain

From BEGINNER BOOKS A Division of Random House, Inc.

Copyright © 1985 by Berenstains, Inc. All rights reserved under International and Pan-American Copyright Conventions. Published in the United States by Random House, Inc., New York, and simultaneously in Canada by Random House of Canada Limited, Toronto. *Library of Congress Cataloging in Publication Data:* Berenstain, Stan. The Berenstain bears on the moon. (A Bright & early book ; BE 27) SUMMARY: Two Berenstain Bears and their pup take a rocket ship to the moon. 1. Children's stories, American. [1. Moon—Exploration— Fiction. 2. Bears—Fiction. 3. Stories in rhyme] I. Berenstain, Jan. II. Title. III. Series. PZ8.3.B4493Bhi 1985 [E] 84-20428 ISBN: 0-394-87180-4 (trade); 0-394-97180-9 (lib. bdg.)
Manufactured in the United States of America   1 2 3 4   J K L

On the night before
the Bears' big day,
they look at the moon,
far, far away.

Then morning comes.
Today is the day
they will go to the moon,
far, far away.

10-9-8-7-6-5-4-3-2-1!

The crowd counts down.
The rockets blast.
They wave good-bye.
They are off at last!

Two little bears
and one little pup.
They are off to the moon,
going up, up, up!

They look back down.
But they can't find
their treehouse home.
They have left it far behind.

Where is their town?
It is hard to say.
Their town is now
far, far away.

Now their feet
no longer touch the ground!
They are out in space.
They float around.

Two floating bears
and their floating hound!

Up ahead!
It's a shower!
It's a meteor shower!
They will have to go through!
Turn on more power!

Will they get to the moon?
They will! They must!
Their slogan is
TO THE MOON OR BUST!

Behind them, the earth
is now so small
it is nothing more
than a small blue ball.

The pup begins
to wonder when
his paws will touch
the earth again.

Then up ahead,
it's there! The moon!
Buckle up tight!
We are landing soon!

Landing!
They are landing
in a cloud of dust.

They said they would.
And they said they must.
They made it to the moon.
And they didn't bust!

Down onto the old moon
they step with pride.
Two bears
and a pup
along for the ride.

Now the bears
have many things to do.
But first they look around.
They enjoy the view.

Then
they fly their flag.

They take moon notes.

They collect moon rocks
in their moon rock totes.

Then they try some jumps.
High in the sky.
Moon jumps
almost make you fly!

Now it's time to get
behind the wheel
and explore the moon
in their moonmobile.

Two bears on the moon.
They are all packed up,
ready to go home now.
So is their pup.

Will their ship lift off?
Will the rockets burn?
Will the two little bears
and their pup return?

If the two little bears
use all their skill,
they will return.
They will! They will!

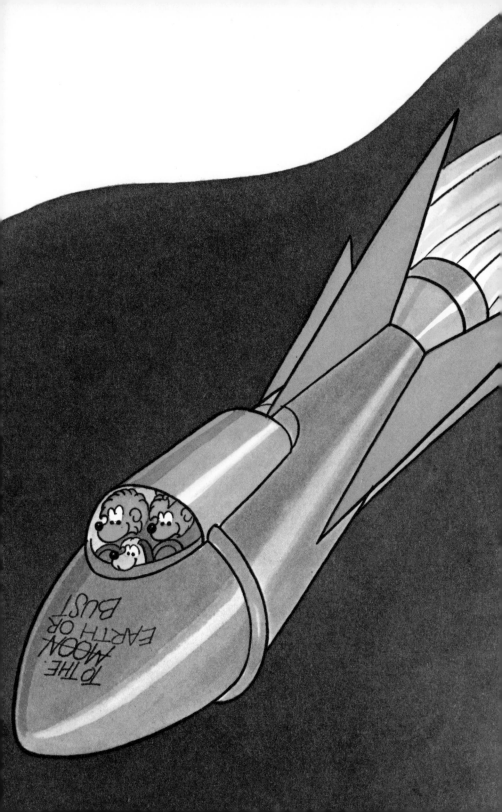

Two bears and their pup
in their rocket ship,
on their way back home
on their back-to-earth trip.

To their friends on the ground!
To their house!
Safe and sound!

Safe back on the earth.
They step out of their ship.
"Wow!" say the bears.
"That was quite a trip!"

Now they look up at the stars,
very, very far away.
Will they go up to a star...?
Well, they may...someday.

Stan and Jan Berenstain

For years Stan and Jan Berenstain were well known to millions of adult readers for their many marvelously funny books and magazine features on family life in America. Then, with *The Big Honey Hunt*, children discovered that they also wrote marvelously funny books about family life in Bear Country. Since then millions of beginning readers have enjoyed the misadventures of the famous Bear family.

The Berenstains went to the same art school (the Philadelphia Museum School), enjoy the same food, tastes, and hobbies, have the same two sons, and as far as can be discovered, type simultaneously on the same typewriter and draw simultaneously on the same piece of paper. They work together in the same studio in Bucks County, Pennsylvania, creating words and pictures that delight bears and children around the world.